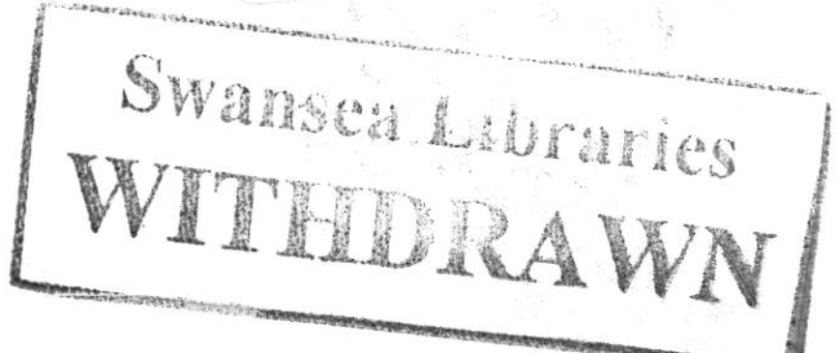

Magical Story Collection

ORCHARD BOOKS

First published in 2014 in Italy by Fivestore
First published in Great Britain in 2016 by The Watts Publishing Group

1 3 5 7 9 10 8 6 4 2

A CIP catalogue record for this book is available from the British Library.

ISBN 978 1 40834 476 7

Printed and bound in China

Orchard Books
An imprint of Hachette Children's Group
Part of The Watts Publishing Group Limited
Carmelite House
50 Victoria Embankment
London EC4Y 0DZ

An Hachette UK Company
www.hachette.co.uk

www.hachettechildrens.co.uk

Prologue

So much has happened since Twilight Sparkle, Applejack, Fluttershy, Pinkie Pie, Rarity and Rainbow Dash first became friends. The ponies have had lots of exciting adventures together, and each one has taught them an important lesson.

The friends have decided to keep a diary to share their memories, hopes and all that they have learned. One day this diary will help them in a way they could never have imagined . . .

The Tree of Harmony

"Looking good up there, Princess Twilight!" called Applejack.

It was the day before the Summer Sun Celebration, and Twilight Sparkle was trying out her new wings. After Twilight saved her friends by restoring their cutie marks, Princess Celestia had crowned her Princess of Equestria. But being a princess wasn't always easy! Luckily her friends Rarity, Applejack, Fluttershy, Pinkie Pie and Rainbow Dash had all come to Canterlot Castle to help her.

Life at the palace was wonderful, and Twilight was proud to be living there. But her friends would be returning to Ponyville soon, and she was worried: could their special friendship survive when they were apart?

"The six of us are united by the Elements of Harmony," said Applejack. "Nothing will ever change that." Still, Twilight felt sad as she gave her friends a goodbye hug.

The next morning, when Twilight Sparkle awoke, a crowd of puzzled ponies had gathered outside the castle. The sun and moon were both shining in the sky, and dark, spiky clouds hovered on the horizon. News had arrived of strange vines creeping out of the Everfree Forest and covering Equestria. But worst of all, Princess Celestia and Princess Luna had both vanished!

"I don't know what's going on," Twilight told Spike the dragon as they flew to Ponyville, "but I'm sure we're going to need my friends and the Elements of Harmony to stop it."

The pony friends were overjoyed to be reunited. Together, they tried to work out who could be behind the chaos.

"I think I have a pretty good idea who's responsible," said Twilight thoughtfully. She used her magic to summon Discord, the spirit of disharmony.

Discord told Twilight he had nothing to do with the strange happenings. "I'm innocent," he insisted, trying to hide a smile. "Would I lie to you?"

The friends didn't trust the tricky creature. While they were wondering what to do, the wise sorceress Zecora appeared from the forest.

Zecora spoke in rhyme:
"I'm afraid it's a mystery to me as well.
This potion may help – but you must add
a spell."

Twilight used her Alicorn magic. As she drank the potion, she was sent back in time . . .

Twilight discovered that, long ago, Princess Celestia and Princess Luna had taken the Elements of Harmony from the Tree of Harmony. The tree's powerful magic controlled everything that grew in the Everfree Forest.

"Something's happened to the Tree of Harmony," Twilight told her friends. "I think it's in danger."

"Let's go and save it!" the brave ponies chorused.

The Everfree Forest looked dark and menacing. As the ponies crept nervously into the trees, Applejack had a terrible thought. "Princess Celestia and Princess Luna are gone . . ." she said, turning to Twilight Sparkle. "What if something happens to you too?"

"She's right, Twilight," Rainbow Dash agreed. "Equestria needs you."

But Twilight refused to leave her friends. "I don't know what's in there," she told them, "but whatever it is, I know we need to face it together."

At last the ponies found the Tree of Harmony. Its leaves were grey, and vines twisted tightly around its trunk. The friends tried to tear them away, but the vines were too strong.

"The tree's dying!" cried Fluttershy. "How can we save it?"

"We have to give it the power to save itself," Twilight realised. "We have to give it back the Elements of Harmony."

None of the ponies wanted to give up their powerful magic. "The Elements of Harmony are what keep us connected," insisted Applejack.

Twilight reassured them: "The Elements of Harmony brought us together, but it's our friendship that will keep us connected. Friendship is more important and more powerful than any magic."

Her friends knew she was right. Quickly, they handed Twilight their magical Elements. Then Twilight used her magic to place them back in the tree.

The tree glowed brightly as the evil spell was broken. Equestria was saved! The friends watched in amazement as Princess Celestia and Princess Luna appeared from inside the tangle of vines.

"It took great courage to give up the Elements," Princess Celestia told them.

"We are forever in your debt," added Princess Luna.

As the princesses spoke, the glowing tree opened up to reveal a magical chest with six locks.

"It is obviously meant for you!" Princess Celestia told the six friends. "To open it you will need six keys. You must find them together."

When the ponies arrived back in Ponyville, Discord was waiting for them. He finally admitted that he had caused all the trouble.

"I planted some plunderseeds thousands of moons ago to capture Princess Celestia and Princess Luna," he explained with a sigh. "But it seems that the Tree of Harmony had enough magic to keep the seeds from growing until now."

It had been a cruel trick, the ponies agreed, but all was well that ended well – and if Discord tried any more mischief, they would be waiting for him!

Dear Diary,
We can't always be with the ones we love the most, but when we really care for our friends, nothing can keep us apart. True friendship is the spell that makes us strong – it is the greatest magic of all.
Twilight Sparkle,
Rainbow Dash, Pinkie Pie,
Applejack, Fluttershy and Rarity

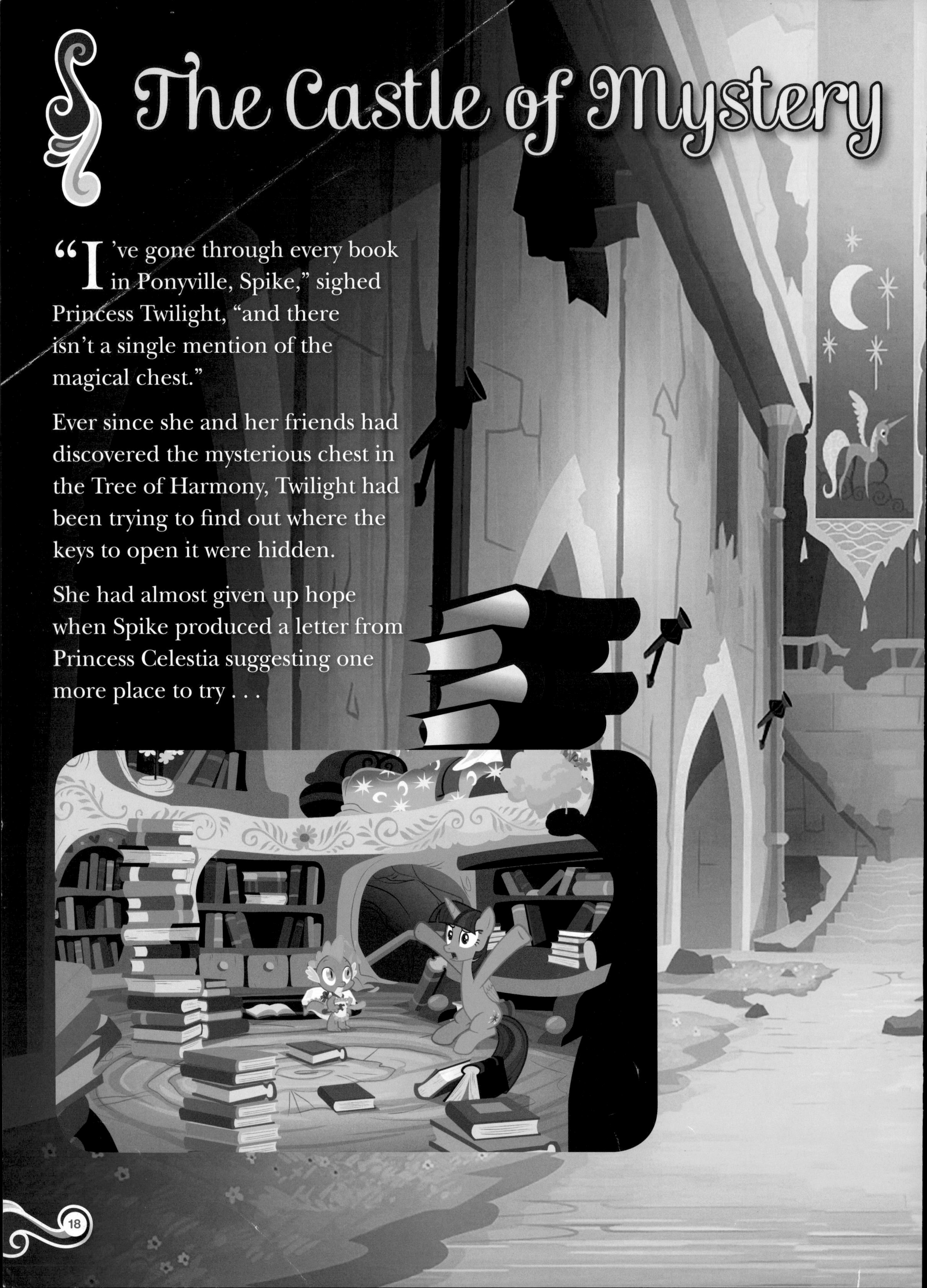

The Castle of Mystery

"I've gone through every book in Ponyville, Spike," sighed Princess Twilight, "and there isn't a single mention of the magical chest."

Ever since she and her friends had discovered the mysterious chest in the Tree of Harmony, Twilight had been trying to find out where the keys to open it were hidden.

She had almost given up hope when Spike produced a letter from Princess Celestia suggesting one more place to try . . .

In the heart of the Everfree Forest was the ancient castle where the princesses Celestia and Luna had once lived. It was now a crumbling ruin, but its library was still there, packed with books from floor to ceiling.

"This place is perfect!" gasped Twilight. She was sure that she would find what she was looking for. Meanwhile Spike tried his best not to be scared of the spiders!

Back in Ponyville, Applejack and Rainbow Dash were trying to find out who was the most daring.

Pinkie Pie was keeping score. "You're both equally daring!" she laughed, as they completed the latest challenge: covering themselves with buzzing bees!

"Then we'll have to come up with another test!" said Rainbow Dash.

Applejack looked at the path leading into the creepy Everfree Forest. "I have an idea . . ." she said, smiling.

Meanwhile, Rarity, Fluttershy and the little bunny Angel were also making their way into the forest. Rarity had heard that the castle was full of ancient tapestries, and she wanted to see them for herself.

"Um, Rarity," whispered Fluttershy. "Are you sure you really need to see those tapestries?"

She was feeling nervous. But Angel hopped on ahead, and his two pony friends followed.

"Well, what's so daring about this place?" Rainbow Dash asked as she and Applejack trotted into the castle.

"According to my granny," said Applejack in a mysterious voice, "when night falls, the castle is haunted by . . . THE PONY OF SHADOWS!"

"I don't believe in ghosts," Rainbow Dash replied, rolling her eyes.

But as the two ponies made their way through the ruins, they both felt a teeny bit frightened. The castle was full of dark corners and spooky passages, and strange sounds echoed through the empty halls.

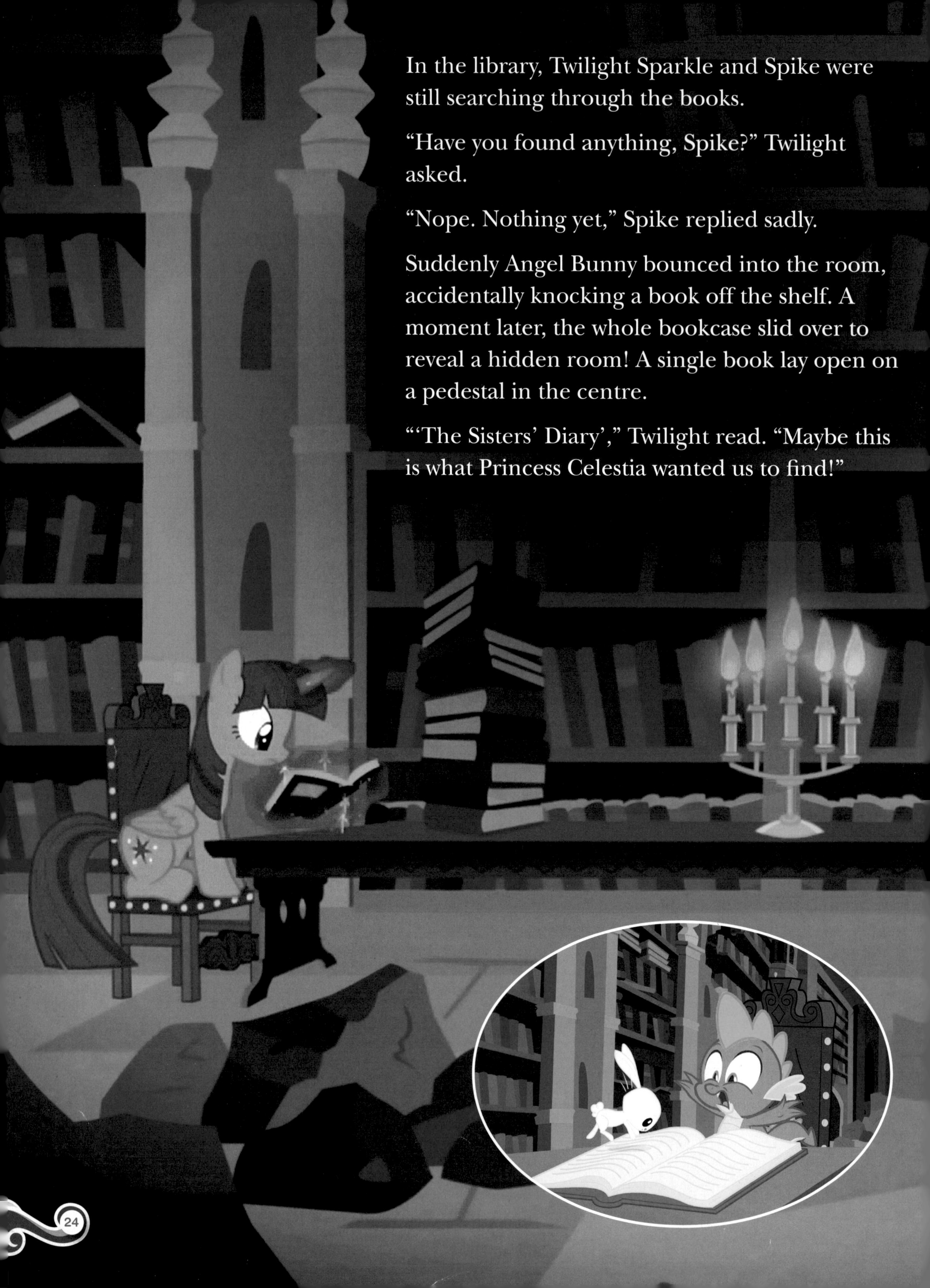

In the library, Twilight Sparkle and Spike were still searching through the books.

"Have you found anything, Spike?" Twilight asked.

"Nope. Nothing yet," Spike replied sadly.

Suddenly Angel Bunny bounced into the room, accidentally knocking a book off the shelf. A moment later, the whole bookcase slid over to reveal a hidden room! A single book lay open on a pedestal in the centre.

"'The Sisters' Diary'," Twilight read. "Maybe this is what Princess Celestia wanted us to find!"

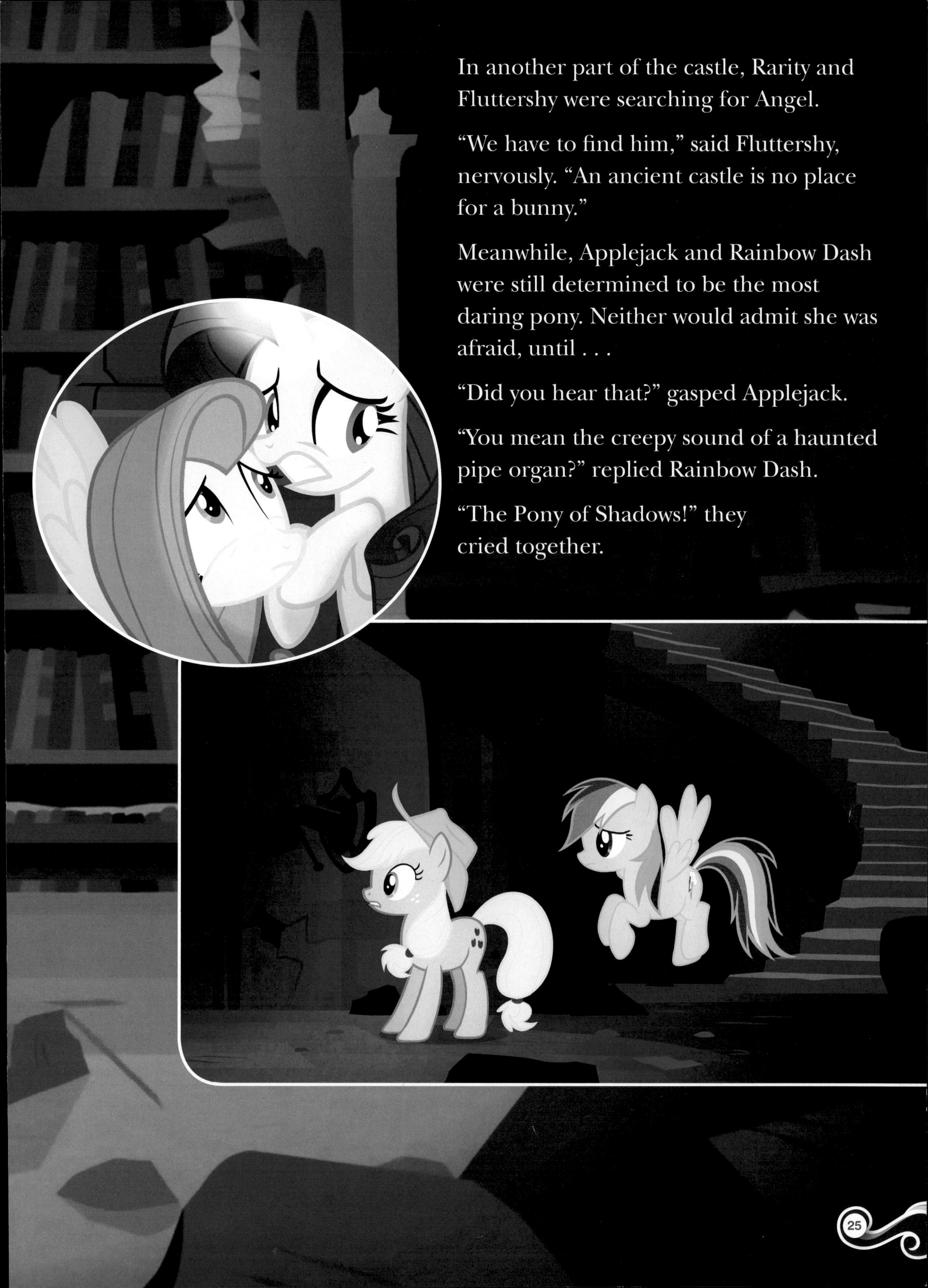

In another part of the castle, Rarity and Fluttershy were searching for Angel.

"We have to find him," said Fluttershy, nervously. "An ancient castle is no place for a bunny."

Meanwhile, Applejack and Rainbow Dash were still determined to be the most daring pony. Neither would admit she was afraid, until . . .

"Did you hear that?" gasped Applejack.

"You mean the creepy sound of a haunted pipe organ?" replied Rainbow Dash.

"The Pony of Shadows!" they cried together.

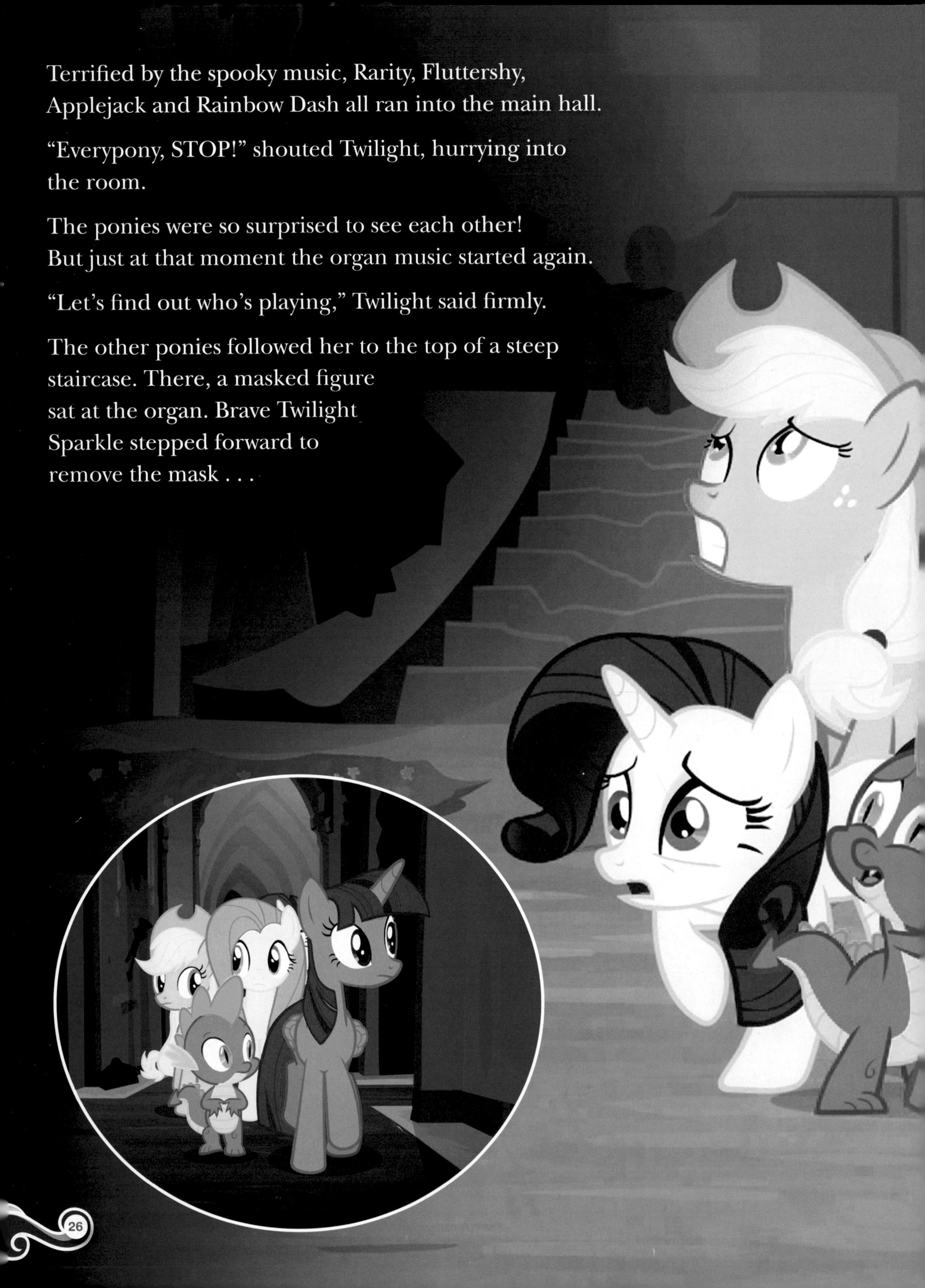

Terrified by the spooky music, Rarity, Fluttershy, Applejack and Rainbow Dash all ran into the main hall.

"Everypony, STOP!" shouted Twilight, hurrying into the room.

The ponies were so surprised to see each other! But just at that moment the organ music started again.

"Let's find out who's playing," Twilight said firmly.

The other ponies followed her to the top of a steep staircase. There, a masked figure sat at the organ. Brave Twilight Sparkle stepped forward to remove the mask . . .

"PINKIE PIE!" the friends chorused.

"*You're* the Pony of Shadows?" said Applejack, puzzled.

"The pony of what?" Pinkie Pie replied. "I saw you all go into the castle and I just thought I'd add a little music to the party!"

The friends laughed as they realised how they had let their imaginations run away with them.

The ponies explained why they had each come to the castle, and Twilight showed them the princesses' diary.

Suddenly she had a great idea. "Why don't *we* keep a diary?" she exclaimed. "Just like the Royal Pony Sisters? We can learn from each other. And maybe one day other ponies will read it and learn something too."

"What a splendid idea!" said Rarity, and the other ponies all agreed.

As the six pony friends, Angel and Spike set off back to Ponyville, Applejack smiled. "I know what my first diary entry will be," she said: "*Dear Diary, I'm glad Granny's story wasn't true.*"

"I never believed that silly story," muttered Rainbow Dash.

But from the darkness of the castle . . .

. . . two yellow eyes watched the ponies go.

Perhaps Granny's stories weren't so ridiculous after all!

Dear Diary,

Today I learned that sometimes our imaginations can run away with us. But when they do, true friends can help us see things as they really are.

Your very brave,
Rainbow Dash

The Ponyville Days Festival

Everypony in Ponyville was very excited. In three days' time, the town would hold its Ponyville Days Festival, and Mayor Mare was about to announce who had been chosen as the Pony of Ceremonies.

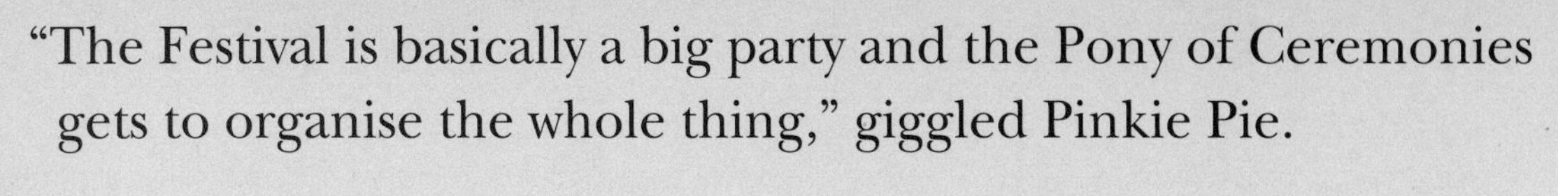

"The Festival is basically a big party and the Pony of Ceremonies gets to organise the whole thing," giggled Pinkie Pie.

The mayor began to speak. "Citizens of Ponyville, this year's Ponyville Days Pony of Ceremonies is . . . Rarity!"

The ponies gathered round to congratulate Rarity.

“The theme I’ve chosen is Small Town Chic,” said Rarity. “Show them, Spike.”

“There will be a Ponyville gala in the town square,” announced Spike, pointing to Rarity’s sketches. “And, of course, a Ponyville fashion show.”

“It has to be perfect,” said Rarity, sighing dreamily, “because we have a very important guest to impress: the amazingly handsome and talented Trenderhoof – he’s coming to write about the festival.”

The friends worked hard to get Ponyville ready for the festival, and soon the town was looking fabulous. As the Friendship Express rolled into Ponyville Station, Rarity waited nervously.

At last, a handsome pony with a perfectly styled mane stepped on to the platform.

"Um . . . Hi. Ahem. Hello, Mr Trenderhoof," stammered Rarity. "Welcome to Ponyville."

"Please, call me Trend," said the new arrival, giving Rarity a dazzling smile.

Rarity showed Trend the sights of Ponyville and told him all about her plans for the festival.

"I'm so glad to be here, Rarity," said Trend, flashing her another smile. "I'm sure your event will be a huge success."

As the pair arrived at Sweet Apple Acres, Rarity had never felt so happy. It seemed that Trend liked her as much as she liked him!

But suddenly, Trend stopped in his tracks. “Who is that?” he gasped. “She’s the most beautiful pony I’ve ever seen!”

Rarity turned around in surprise. She saw Applejack, busy collecting apples. Trenderhoof was staring at Applejack with a dreamy look on his face.

Rarity rushed back to the Carousel Boutique, where she told Spike what had happened. “Trend doesn’t like me,” she sobbed, gazing sadly at her Trenderhoof posters. “He likes Applejack. What does she have that I don’t?”

Meanwhile, on the farm, Applejack wished Trenderhoof would leave her alone. "I'm kinda busy," she told him, "and if I can't get my chores done, there won't be a Ponyville Days Festival for you to write about!"

"Don't worry!" cried a voice. "I'm here to help!"

Applejack turned round and saw Rarity. She was wearing a brand-new farm pony outfit, complete with sequined straw hat and boots. Applejack stared at her friend in amazement.

Rarity knew she should be busy organising the festival, but she was sure that if Trenderhoof saw her working on the farm like a real country pony, he'd realise she was the pony for him.

But Trenderhoof had other ideas. "Rarity?" he asked. "Do you think Applejack would be my date for the festival?"

Rarity's heart sank to her boots. "I don't know," she sighed.

Later that day, when Applejack ducked into the barn to hide from Trenderhoof, she was surprised to find Rarity there.

Rarity stamped her hoof angrily. “It should be *me* that Trend likes, not you,” she told Applejack.

“I’m not interested in him!” said Applejack. “And shouldn’t you be getting ready for the festival instead of trying to impress Trenderhoof?”

“Actually, I have a new vision for the festival, and Trend’s going to love it,” said Rarity. “Just you wait and see!”

When Rarity reappeared, the ponies were shocked to see her wearing patched overalls and a battered straw hat. “The new theme for the festival is Simple Ways,” she announced.

“Rarity, this isn’t you!” said Twilight Sparkle. “You like fashion and fancy things.”

And she wasn’t the only one who didn’t look like herself. When Applejack arrived, she was wearing a beautiful jewelled gown, with her hair in a fancy style! Applejack hoped that her plan to help Rarity would work . . .

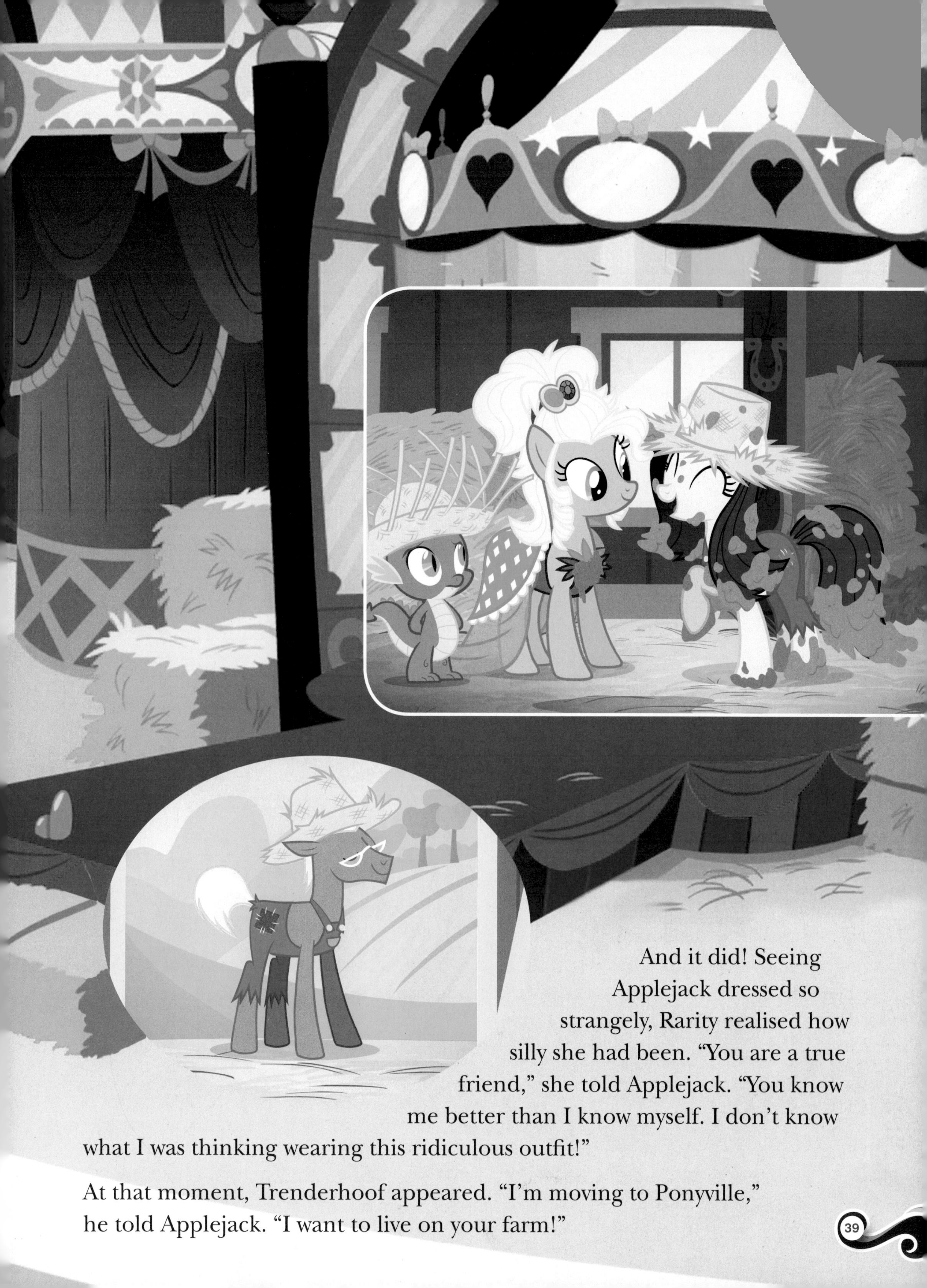

And it did! Seeing Applejack dressed so strangely, Rarity realised how silly she had been. "You are a true friend," she told Applejack. "You know me better than I know myself. I don't know what I was thinking wearing this ridiculous outfit!"

At that moment, Trenderhoof appeared. "I'm moving to Ponyville," he told Applejack. "I want to live on your farm!"

Applejack was speechless, so Rarity stepped in to help her.

"I think what Applejack wants to say is that nopony should change themselves just to impress somepony else," she told Trenderhoof. "If somepony doesn't like you for who you are, it's their loss."

Leaving Trenderhoof to think about what she'd said, Rarity dashed off to make her final preparations for the festival. There was still time to put everything right!

All of Ponyville turned out to enjoy the festival, and even Trenderhoof had a wonderful time. Everyone agreed that it had been the most elegant Ponyville Days Festival ever, all thanks to Ponyville's most stylish Pony of Ceremonies, Rarity – with a little help from her friends!

Dear Diary,

Nopony can be liked by everypony – and that's the way it should be. True friends like you for who you are, and changing yourself to impress them is no way to make new ones. And, actually, when you are as fabulous as I am . . . it's practically a crime!

Affectionately yours,
Rarity

Attack of the Bats!

"Yee-haw!" laughed Applejack. "It's officially apple-bucking day!"

The excited pony couldn't wait to start picking all the delicious, ripe apples in her orchard.

But when Applejack knocked her first apple from the tree, instead of being sweet and juicy, it was rotten and soft. There could be only one reason . . . "Vampire Fruit Bats!" she gasped.

Applejack rushed to tell her friends the terrible news. "Vampire Fruit Bats are attacking Sweet Apple Acres!" she cried. "They'll ruin the whole crop."

"They're only here because they're hungry," said gentle Fluttershy.

"They're pests," said Applejack. "They'd better not try eating my enormous prize apple. It's our entry for the Appaloosa Fair Apple Competition. Sweet Apple Acres has won every year since the competition began!"

Fluttershy decided to try talking to the bats.

"Um, excuse me, Mr Vampire Fruit Bat. We were just wondering if, maybe, you wouldn't mind leaving that really big apple alone?"

But the bats kept on slurping.

"If we built a sanctuary for them, with their own apples to enjoy, they'd leave ours alone," suggested Fluttershy.

But her friends were not convinced.

"Those bats have got to go!" said Applejack firmly.

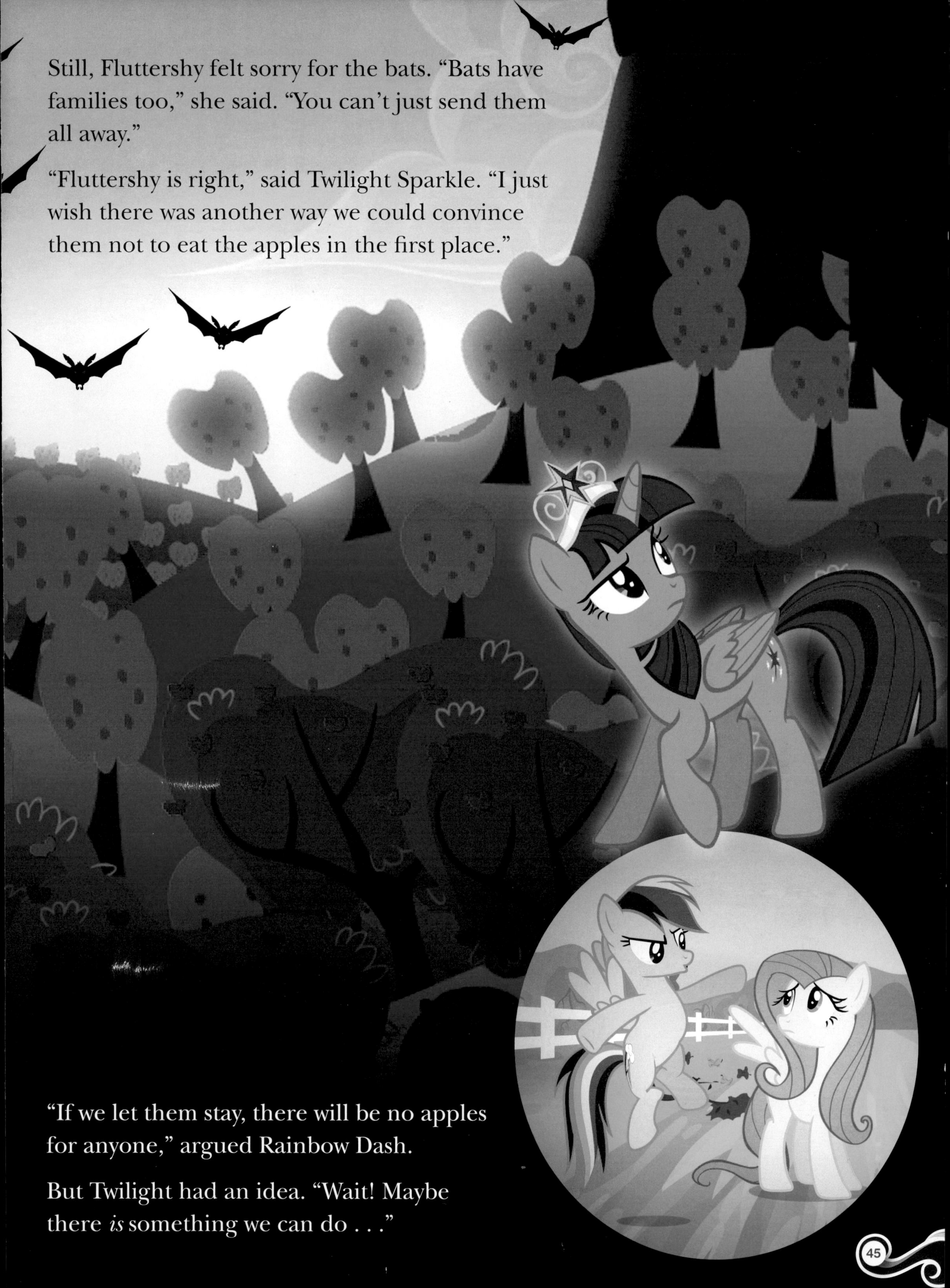

Still, Fluttershy felt sorry for the bats. "Bats have families too," she said. "You can't just send them all away."

"Fluttershy is right," said Twilight Sparkle. "I just wish there was another way we could convince them not to eat the apples in the first place."

"If we let them stay, there will be no apples for anyone," argued Rainbow Dash.

But Twilight had an idea. "Wait! Maybe there *is* something we can do . . ."

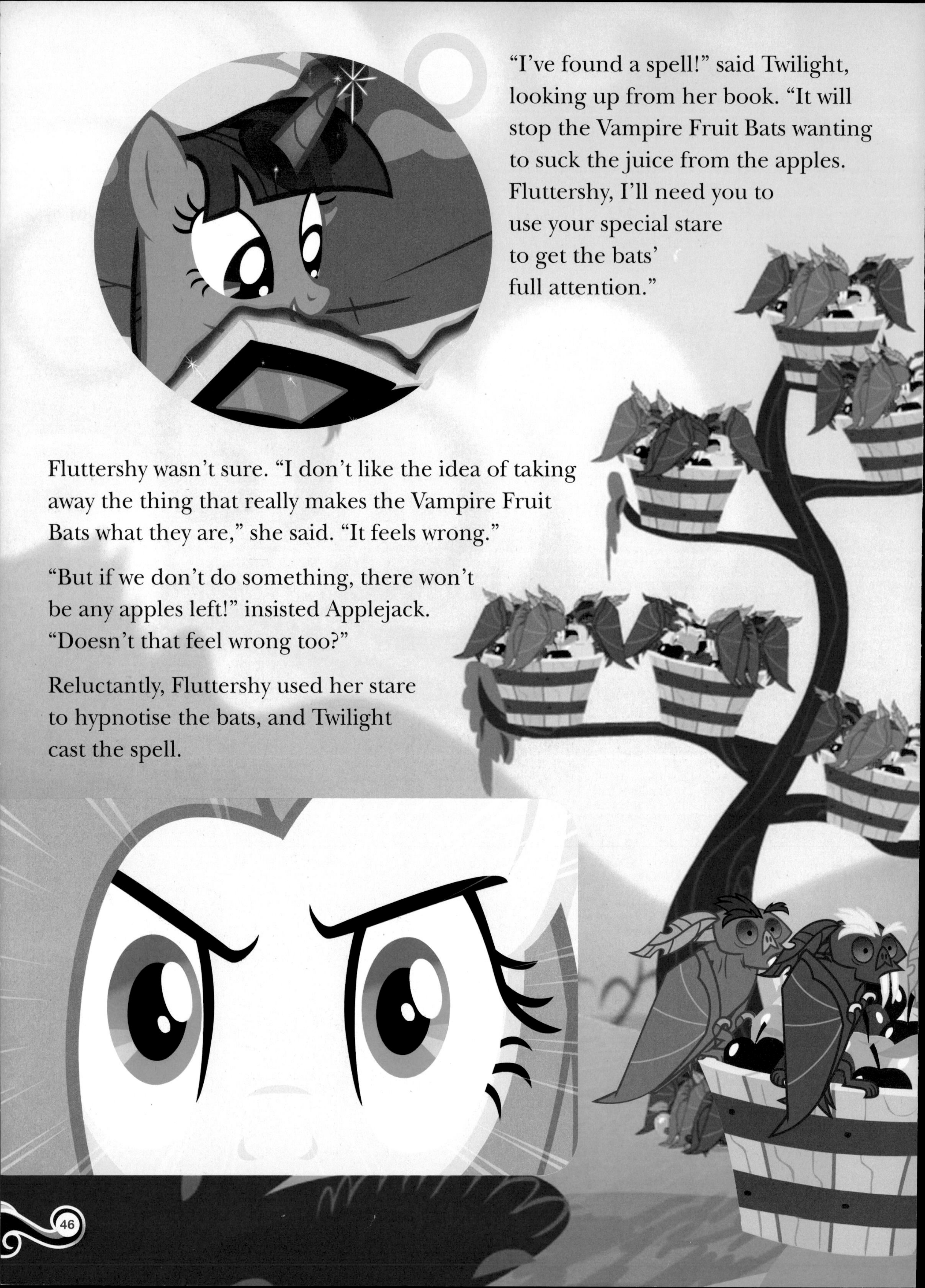

"I've found a spell!" said Twilight, looking up from her book. "It will stop the Vampire Fruit Bats wanting to suck the juice from the apples. Fluttershy, I'll need you to use your special stare to get the bats' full attention."

Fluttershy wasn't sure. "I don't like the idea of taking away the thing that really makes the Vampire Fruit Bats what they are," she said. "It feels wrong."

"But if we don't do something, there won't be any apples left!" insisted Applejack. "Doesn't that feel wrong too?"

Reluctantly, Fluttershy used her stare to hypnotise the bats, and Twilight cast the spell.

Rainbow Dash tried offering one of the bats a juicy apple. The bat turned away, disgusted.

"Whoo-ee! The spell worked. My crop is saved!" cried Applejack.

"I have a bad feeling about this," said Fluttershy.

As the day went on, her bad feeling got stronger and stronger. Then when night fell, a terrible transformation took place. Fluttershy became . . . Flutterbat!

The friends were horrified when they saw Fluttershy the Flutterbat hanging upside down from one of the apple trees.

"How did this happen?" gasped Rarity.

"My spell must have backfired," said Twilight Sparkle. "It took the Vampire Fruit Bats' desire to be Vampire Fruit Bats and gave it to Fluttershy instead. We have to reverse the spell to put things right!"

But it wasn't going to be easy.

"Look out!" warned Applejack. The ponies dived to the ground as the Flutterbat swooped down on them at top speed.

They watched anxiously as the Flutterbat flew from tree to tree, slurping up every drop of apple juice and leaving a trail of sucked apples behind her.

"If she carries on like this, there won't be a single apple left," said Rainbow Dash.

"Never mind the apples," replied Applejack. "I just want my friend back."

"If only we had Fluttershy to do her stare on the Flutterbat . . ." sighed Pinkie Pie.

"That's it!" cried Twilight Sparkle. "I've got a plan. We'll need Applejack's giant apple . . ."

"She's coming!" whispered Rainbow Dash.

The Flutterbat dived down towards the enormous apple, but just as she was about to pounce . . .

"Now!" cried Applejack, and the friends pushed the apple aside, revealing a large golden mirror.

The Flutterbat stared into the mirror, hypnotised by her own reflection. Quickly, Twilight Sparkle used her magic to reverse the spell.

As the spell began to work, the Flutterbat spun faster and faster in a blaze of light. Twilight, Applejack, Pinkie Pie, Rainbow Dash, Rarity and Spike watched as the bat-pony changed back into their friend. Then they all rushed to hug Fluttershy.

"I'm so sorry, Fluttershy," said Applejack. "If we'd built the bat sanctuary like you suggested, none of this would have happened."

"Let's build the sanctuary now," said Fluttershy, smiling.

The sanctuary was a huge success. Once Twilight Sparkle had cast a spell to give the Vampire Fruit Bats back their love of apples, the bats all settled down happily into their new home.

"Now we just need to get that apple to the Appaloosa Fair," said Applejack. "I've got a competition to win!"

Dear Diary,

It's important to stand up for what you believe in, and you shouldn't let anypony pressure you into doing something you don't think is right. Sometimes you might have to say "no" to your closest friends, but real friends will always respect you for staying true to yourself.

Sincerely yours,
Fluttershy

Twilight's Kingdom

"All I seem to do these days is smile and wave," sighed Twilight Sparkle.

Princess Twilight had travelled to the Crystal Empire to help Celestia and the other princesses, but she was feeling disappointed by her new royal duties.

"Princess Celestia raises the sun. Princess Luna raises the moon. Princess Cadance protects the Crystal Empire. Is there nothing important for me to do?" she asked.

"Don't worry. You'll soon play your part," Princess Celestia reassured her.

Princess Celestia told Twilight that Equestria was facing a terrible threat.

Long ago, the wicked Lord Tirek and his brother, Scorpan, had tried to steal Equestria's magic. But Scorpan had become a friend of the ponies and told them of his brother's plans.

"Tirek was sent to Tartarus for his crimes," Celestia explained, "but he has escaped and returned to Equestria. By stealing magic, he has increased his dark powers."

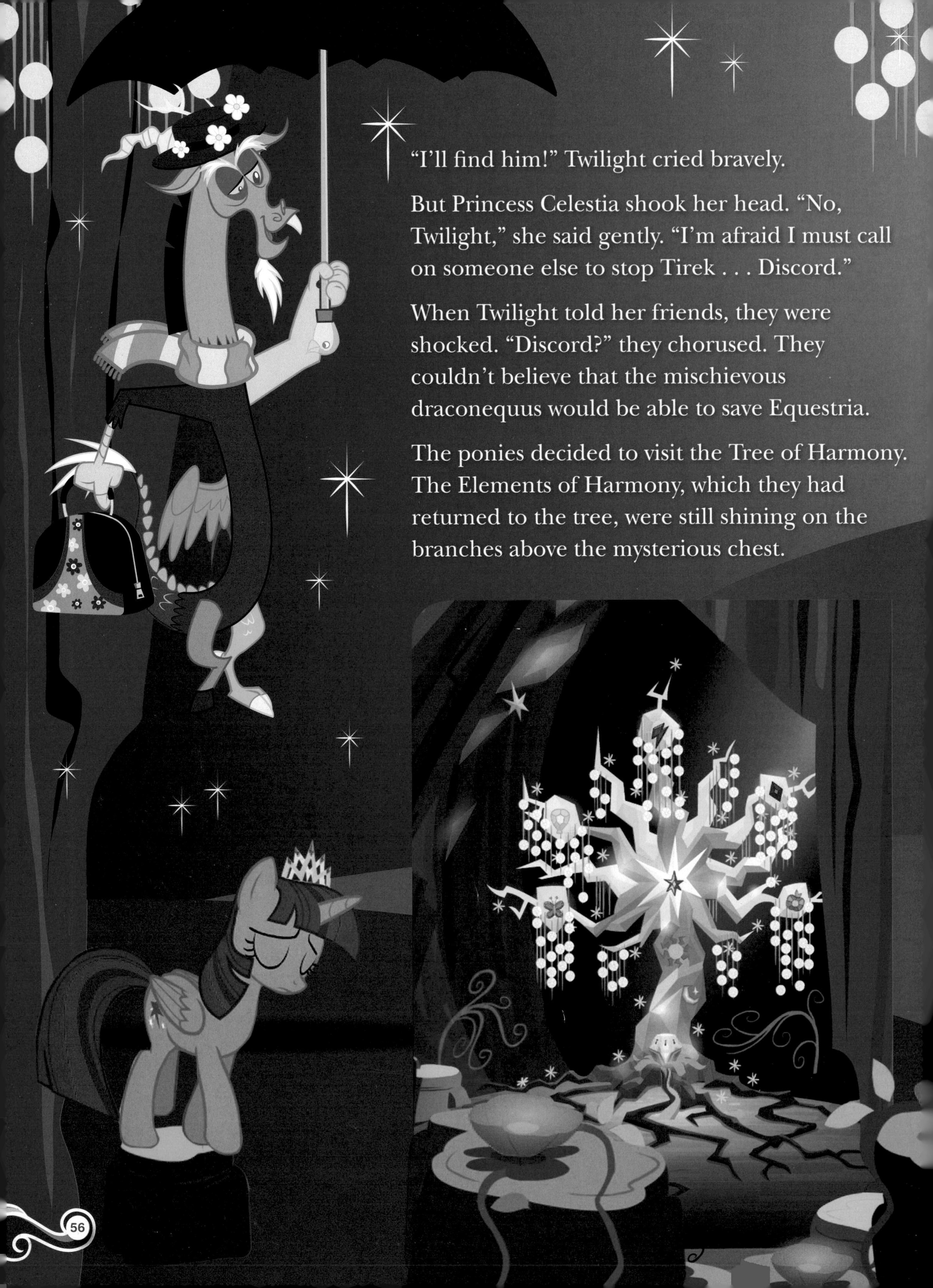

"I'll find him!" Twilight cried bravely.

But Princess Celestia shook her head. "No, Twilight," she said gently. "I'm afraid I must call on someone else to stop Tirek . . . Discord."

When Twilight told her friends, they were shocked. "Discord?" they chorused. They couldn't believe that the mischievous draconequus would be able to save Equestria.

The ponies decided to visit the Tree of Harmony. The Elements of Harmony, which they had returned to the tree, were still shining on the branches above the mysterious chest.

As the friends stood gazing at the beautiful tree, Discord appeared. "I'm heading off on my extremely important mission," he said, looking smug. "I see you still haven't unlocked that chest of yours. What if there's something inside that could help Twilight prove her royal worth? Who knows, maybe there's something in that diary you've all been writing that will help you open it."

And with that, Discord snapped his claws and disappeared.

Back in the old castle library, Twilight turned the pages of the diary, reading carefully. “I think I’ve found something!” she exclaimed suddenly.

“What is it, Twi?” asked Applejack.

Twilight looked at her friends. “Since we first met, you have each had a tough choice to make,” she explained. “When you made the right choice and embraced your Element, it helped somepony else, who gave you an object to thank you. Perhaps those gifts are the key to opening the chest!”

Quickly, the ponies took their gifts to the chest. As they held the objects up, beams of rainbow light shone from the keyholes and each gift was transformed into a key. But there was one key missing . . . Twilight had not yet earned a gift.

Just then, Twilight was summoned back to Canterlot Palace. Celestia, Luna and Cadance were waiting for her.

"Discord has betrayed the ponies of Equestria and joined forces with Lord Tirek," Princess Celestia told her. "With Discord's help, Tirek has stolen magic from the flying Pegasi and the Earth Ponies. Now he wants our Alicorn magic."

"We must give our magic to you, Twilight, before Tirek steals it," Princess Luna continued. "Tirek doesn't know that you are the fourth Alicorn princess, so he will not know where the magic has gone."

"But I'm still learning to control my own Alicorn magic," said Twilight. "How can I take on even more?"

"You represent the Element of Magic," Princess Cadance reassured her. "You can do this."

Princess Twilight knew it was her duty to help save Equestria. The brave little pony took a deep breath and, in a dazzling flash of white, the three other princesses transferred all their powers to her.

The next day, Tirek and Discord stormed into Canterlot Castle. When Tirek realised the princesses no longer had any magic, he laughed. "Now there is nothing anyone can do to stop me!"

"Don't you mean mean *us*?" said Discord, starting to feel worried.

"Of course," said Tirek, with a sly smile. He took a gold medallion from around his neck and gave it to Discord. "I give you this medal as a sign of my gratitude and loyalty," he told him.

Discord was so pleased that he blurted out, "There is a fourth Alicorn princess in Ponyville! It's Princess Twilight Sparkle!"

"You must find her!" growled Tirek.

Discord knew that the best way to get to Twilight was through her friends. He trapped them in a cage and Tirek stole their magic. To Discord's dismay, Tirek then stole his magic too!

"You're no use to me now that I know Princess Twilight's secret," Tirek laughed.

Discord had been betrayed. Without his magic there was nothing more he could do. Only Princess Twilight could save Equestria now.

When Twilight arrived to rescue her friends, Tirek was waiting for her. He threw bolts of magic towards Twilight, which destroyed everything they touched. Twilight Sparkle responded with her own powerful shots of magic.

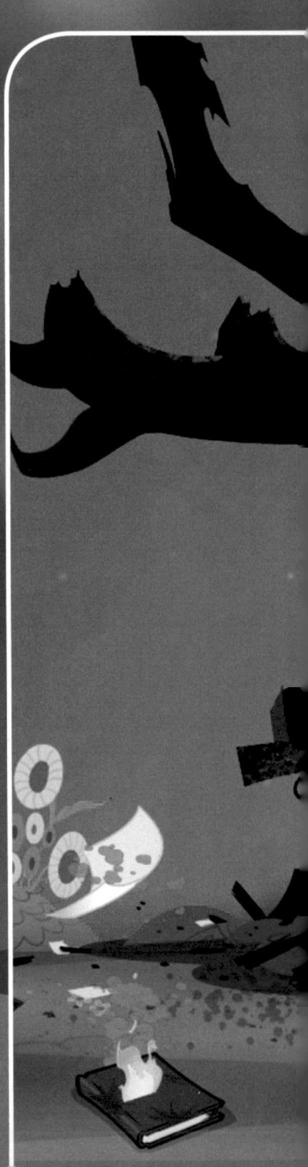

"Give up your magic, Princess," Tirek demanded. "Then I will release your friends." He pointed to the ponies.

"I will give you my magic in exchange for *all* my friends," said Twilight, pointing to Discord.

"He has betrayed you, but you still call him a friend?" laughed Tirek.

As he took Twilight's magic, Tirek grew to an enormous size. It seemed that Equestria was lost.

Discord couldn't believe that Twilight had given up her power to help him. He handed her the medallion that Tirek had offered him. "Twilight, please take this as a sign of our true friendship."

The ponies gasped. Could this be the last gift they needed to open the chest?

The friends raced to the Tree of Harmony. As Twilight held the medallion up to the chest, it transformed into the final key. The chest flew open and a ray of rainbow light shot out, swirling round the ponies and lifting them into the air above Tirek.

"This is impossible!" cried Tirek as he began to shrink. "You have no magic!"

"You're wrong!" said Twilight. "I may have given you my Alicorn magic, but I still hold the most powerful magic of all – the Magic of Friendship."

In a blast of light, the evil Tirek vanished for ever, and all the magic he had stolen was returned to its rightful keepers. Equestria was saved!

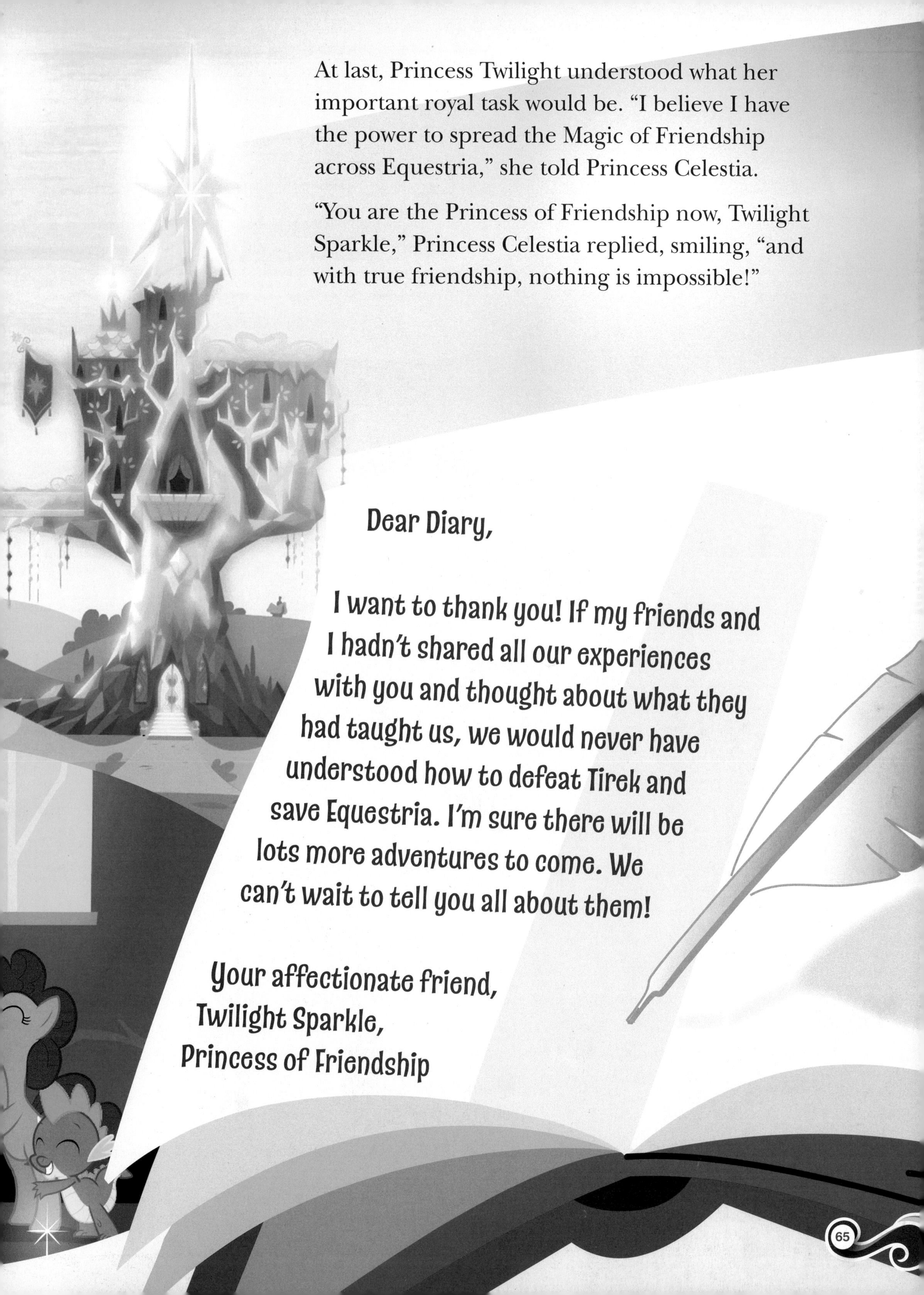

At last, Princess Twilight understood what her important royal task would be. "I believe I have the power to spread the Magic of Friendship across Equestria," she told Princess Celestia.

"You are the Princess of Friendship now, Twilight Sparkle," Princess Celestia replied, smiling, "and with true friendship, nothing is impossible!"

Dear Diary,

I want to thank you! If my friends and I hadn't shared all our experiences with you and thought about what they had taught us, we would never have understood how to defeat Tirek and save Equestria. I'm sure there will be lots more adventures to come. We can't wait to tell you all about them!

Your affectionate friend,
Twilight Sparkle,
Princess of Friendship

Discover more spellbinding stories from My Little Pony!

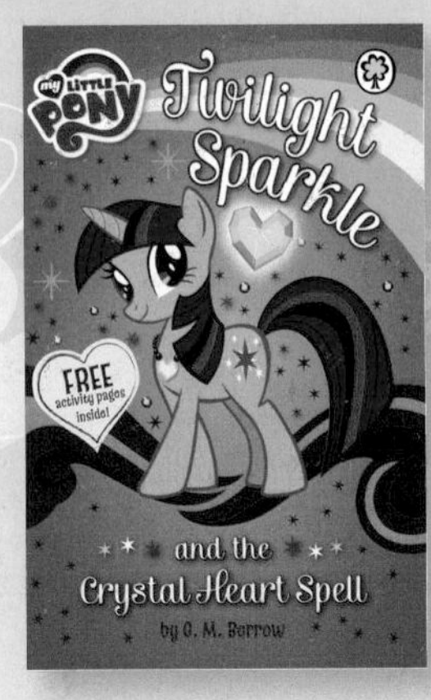

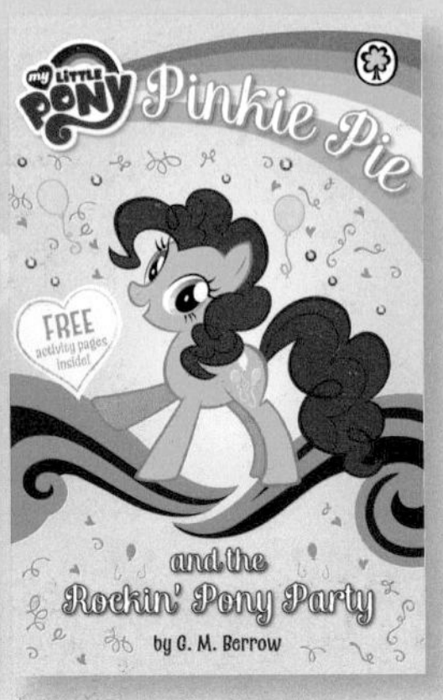

Orchard books are available from all good bookshops.
They can be ordered via our website: www.orchardbooks.co.uk,
or by telephone: 01235 827 702, or fax: 01235 827 703